P9-EMG-508

Pp

Pablo, His Papa, and the Letter **P**

Alphabet Friends

by Cynthia Klingel and Robert B. Noyed

Published in the United States of America by The Child's World®
P.O. Box 326
Chanhassen, MN 55317-0326
800-599-READ
www.childsworld.com

The Child's World®: Mary Berendes, Publishing Director

Editorial Directions, Inc.: E. Russell Primm, Editorial Director; Emily Dolbear, Line Editor; Ruth Martin, Editorial Assistant; Linda S. Koutris, Photo Researcher and Selector

Photographs ©: Thinkstock/Getty Images: Cover & 9; Photodisc/Getty Images: 10, 13; Corbis: 14, 17; Jonathan Blair/Corbis: 18; Emanuele Taroni/Photodisc/Getty Images: 21.

Library of Congress Cataloging-in-Publication Data
Klingel, Cynthia Fitterer.
Pablo, his papa, and the letter P / by Cynthia Klingel and Robert B. Noyed.
p. cm. – (Alphabet readers)
Summary: A simple story about a boy named Pablo and the presents his papa sends him introduce the letter "p".
ISBN 1-59296-106-1 (Library Bound : alk. paper)
[1. Gifts–Fiction. 2. Fathers and sons–Fiction. 3. Alphabet.] I. Noyed, Robert B. II. Title. III. Series.
PZ7.K6798Pab 2003
[E]–dc21 2003006602

Note to parents and educators:
The first skill children acquire before becoming successful readers is individual letter recognition. The Alphabet Friends series has been created with the needs of young learners in mind. Each engaging book begins by showing the difference between the capital letter and the lowercase letter. In each of the books on the vowels and the consonants c and g, children are introduced to the different sounds that the letter can make. Finally, children see that the letters can be found at the beginning of a word, in the middle of a word, and in most cases, at the end of a word.

Following the introduction, children meet their Alphabet Friends. The friend in each story encounters many words that include the featured letter of that book. Each noun that begins with the title letter is highlighted in red with the initial letter of the word in bold. Above the word is a rebus drawing that establishes a strong picture cue.

At the end of each book, we have included three words lists. Can your young learners find all the words in each book with the title letter in them?

Let's learn about the letter **P.**

The letter **P** can look like this: **P.**

The letter **P** can also look like this: **p.**

The letter **p** can be at the

beginning of a word, like party.

party

The letter **p** can be in the

middle of a word, like ape.

a**p**e

The letter **p** can be at the end of a word, like lamp.

lam**p**

The postal worker knocked on **P**ablo's door. She had a **p**ackage for **P**ablo!

The **p**ackage was from **P**apa. **P**apa

was on a trip to **P**aris. He went on an

airplane. **P**ablo was excited to see

what was in the **p**ackage.

Pablo opened the **p**ackage. He pulled

out a **p**ostcard. **P**apa had printed "See

you soon!" on the **p**ostcard.

POST
CARD

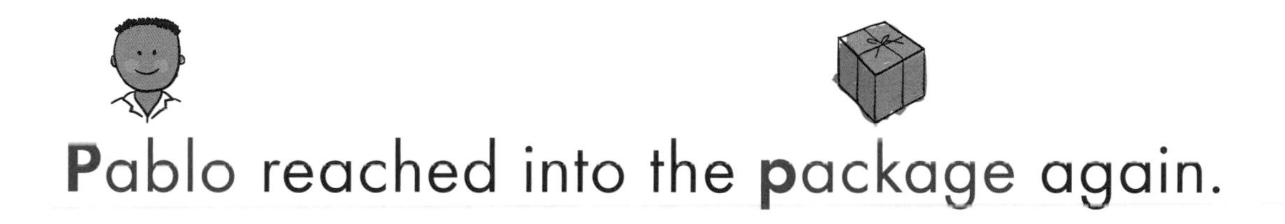

Pablo reached into the **p**ackage again.

He pulled out a toy animal. It was a

panda. **P**apa saw **p**andas on his trip.

Pablo was pleased. He had many pretend

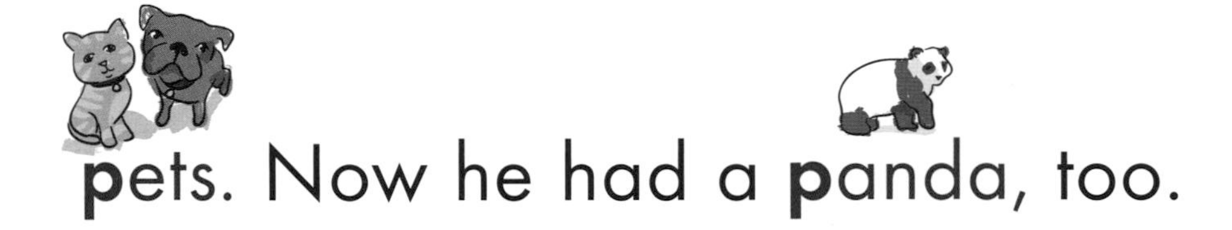

pets. Now he had a **p**anda, too.

Yankees

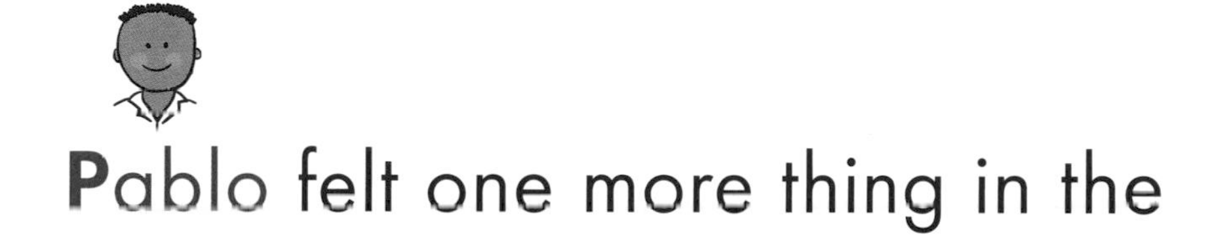

Pablo felt one more thing in the

package. He pulled out a pair of purple

flip-flops. What was **P**apa thinking?

Soon **P**apa will be coming home on the airplane. **P**ablo will have a **p**arty to welcome **P**apa home. **P**apa will be proud.

Fun Facts

When you think of a panda, do you think of a large, black-and-white animal that looks like a bear? If so, you are thinking of a giant panda. But there is another kind of panda, called the red panda. The red panda is much smaller and looks more like a raccoon or a fox than a bear. In fact, scientists argue about whether pandas are part of the bear family, the raccoon family, or a family all their own. Both kinds of pandas live on steep mountains in Asia and eat bamboo. Sadly, the giant panda is an endangered animal. There are only about 1,000 giant pandas living in the wild.

Paris is a city in northern France. It is the capital and largest city of the country. Paris is often called the "City of Lights" because of its magical beauty. Millions of people visit Paris every year because of its wonderful gardens, parks, restaurants, museums, palaces, and monuments. The Eiffel Tower is the city's most popular tourist attraction.

To Read More

About the Letter P

Flanagan, Alice K. *A Pet: The Sound of P.* Chanhassen, Minn.: The Child's World, 2000.

About Pandas

Amato, Carol A., and David Wenzel. *The Giant Panda: Hope for Tomorrow.* Hauppauge, N.Y.: Barrons, 2000.

Butler, John. *Pi-shu: The Little Panda.* Atlanta: Peachtree Publishers, 2000.

Petty, Kate. *Pandas.* New York: Franklin Watts, 1990.

Rutten, Joshua. *Red Pandas.* Chanhassen, Minn.: The Child's World, 1998.

About Paris

Cazet, Denys. *Minnie and Moo Go to Paris.* New York: DK Publishing, 1999.

Thompson, Kay, and Hilary Knight. *Eloise in Paris.* New York: Simon and Schuster, 1957.

Words with P

Words with P at the Beginning

Pablo
Pablo's
package
pair
panda
pandas
papa
Paris
party
pets
pleased
postal
postcard
pretend
printed
proud
pulled
purple

Words with P in the Middle

airplane
ape
flip-flops
opened
papa

Words with P at the End

flip-flop
lamp
trip

About the Authors

Cynthia Klingel has worked as a high school English teacher and an elementary teacher. She is currently the curriculum director for a Minnesota school district. Cynthia Klingel lives with her family in Mankato, Minnesota.

Robert B. Noyed started his career as a newspaper reporter. Since then, he has worked in communications and public relations for a Minnesota school district for more than fourteen years. Robert B. Noyed lives with his family in Brooklyn Center, Minnesota.